© 2012 Age of Learning, Inc.

Published by Age of Learning, Inc., P.O. Box 10458, Glendale, California 91209.

No part of this work may be reproduced in whole or in part, or stored in a retrieval system,

or transmitted in any form or by any means, electronic, mechanical, photocopying,

recording, or otherwise, without written permission of the publisher.

ABCmouse.com and associated logos are trademarks and/or

registered trademarks of Age of Learning, Inc.

Library of Congress Cataloging-in-Publication Data

The Cat and the Rat/Age of Learning, Inc.

Summary: In this Word Family Beginning Reader, two animals become friends

and make a trade that benefits each of them.

ISBN: 978-1-62116-013-7

Library of Congress Control Number: 2012912292

21 20 19 18 17 16 15 14 13 12   1 2 3 4 5

Printed in the U.S.A, on 10% recycled paper. ♻

First printing, October 2012

The Cat and the Rat

Age of Learning, Inc., Glendale, California
This book is also available at **ABCmouse.com**, the award-winning early learning online curriculum.
Find free apps at **ABCmouse.com/apps**.

There was a cat
who had a mat.
On the mat
he ate and sat.

He sat and ate!
He ate and sat!

Soon the cat
was very fat!

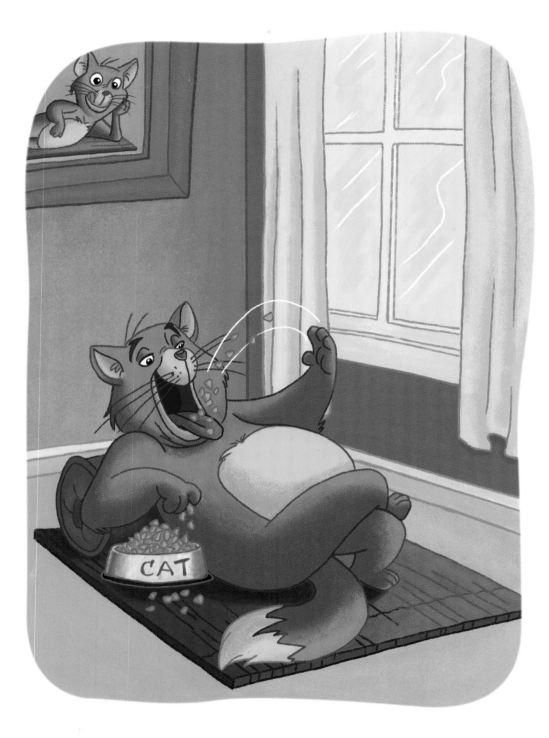

One day, the cat said, "Look at that! I am too fat! I am way too fat!"

"I will get up
from that mat!"

Then the cat
put on his hat.

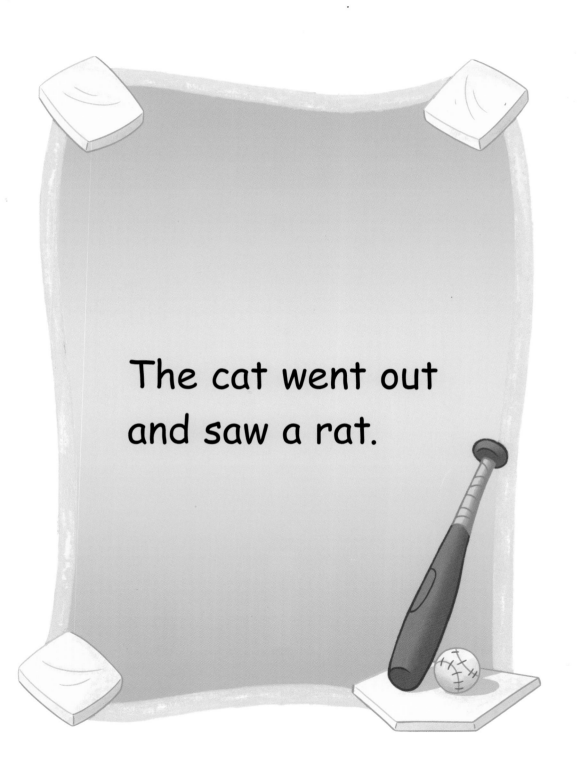

The cat went out
and saw a rat.

"I like that hat!"
said the rat to
the cat.

"I like that bat!"
said the cat
to the rat.

The cat let the rat
put on the hat.

The rat let the cat
swing the bat.

Then the cat said,
"Thank you, rat!
Maybe if I swing
the bat, soon I will
not be too fat!"

The rat let the cat keep the bat.

The cat let the rat keep the hat.

Now the cat is off the mat. Now the cat can swing the bat. Now the cat is not too fat!

The End